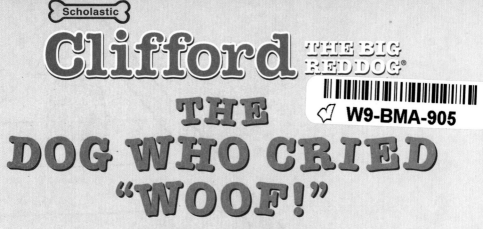

Scholastic

Clifford THE BIG RED DOG®

THE DOG WHO CRIED "WOOF!"

Adapted by Bob Barkly

Illustrated by John Kurtz

W9-BMA-905

Based on the Scholastic book series "Clifford The Big Red Dog" by Norman Bridwell

From the television script "The Dog Who Cried 'Woof'" by Anne-Marie Perrotta and Tean Schultz

Cartwheel
·B·O·O·K·S·®

SCHOLASTIC INC.

New York   Toronto   London   Auckland   Sydney   Mexico City
New Delhi   Hong Kong   Buenos Aires

ISBN 0-439-28978-5

Copyright © 2001 Scholastic Entertainment Inc. All rights reserved. Based on the CLIFFORD THE BIG RED DOG
book series published by Scholastic Inc. TM & © Norman Bridwell.
SCHOLASTIC, CARTWHEEL BOOKS, and associated logos are trademarks and/or registered trademarks of Scholastic Inc.
CLIFFORD, CLIFFORD THE BIG RED DOG, and associated logos are trademarks and/or registered trademarks of Norman Bridwell.

Library of Congress Cataloging-in-Publication Data available

10 9 8 7 6 5 4 3 2 1   01 02 03 04 05

Printed in the U.S.A.   24
First printing, September 2001

"It's a beautiful day," Cleo said. "Let's play tag in the woods."

"Uh...I don't think so,"
Clifford said. "Don't you know
about Stinky the Skunk Ghost?"

"They say he haunts the woods!" T-Bone said.

"He's twenty feet tall.
And he smells as bad as
twenty regular skunks!"

"That's just a story,"

Cleo said.

"Don't you know

Stinky isn't real?"

"Of course we do,"
Clifford said.

"Then what are we
waiting for?" Cleo said.
"Clifford, you be It."

Cleo and T-Bone ran into the woods.

Clifford ran after them.

Cleo was fast....

But Clifford was faster.

He reached out to tag her.

"Look out behind you!" Cleo shouted.

Clifford stopped in his tracks.

So did T-Bone.

"What?" they asked.

"It's Stinky the Skunk
Ghost!" Cleo cried.
Clifford and T-Bone
spun around.
But no one was
behind them.

Cleo fell over laughing.

"I fooled you!"

"That's not funny,"

said T-Bone.

"You scared us."

"I'm sorry," Cleo said.

"But you guys *know*

Stinky's not real.

Let's go swimming."

SPLISH!

SPLASH!

The dogs jumped
into the pond.

"Where is Cleo?"
Clifford asked suddenly.

"She was here a minute
ago," T-Bone said.

Just then, Cleo cried
out from the woods.
"Help! Stinky the Skunk Ghost
has got me!"

Clifford and T-Bone

ran to the rescue.

They found Cleo all alone—

alone and laughing.

"You fooled us again!"

Clifford yelped.

"That wasn't nice."

"It was a joke," Cleo said.

Clifford and T-Bone
were not amused.
They turned
and walked away.

"Don't be mad,"

Cleo called after them.

"I'm sorry."

Cleo tried to catch up

with her friends.

But her bow got caught

on a branch.

"Help!" Cleo cried.

Clifford and T-Bone

kept walking.

They thought Cleo was

playing another trick.

Then they heard

her cry out again.

Cleo sounded really scared.

And something smelled

really bad.

"P-U!" Clifford said.

"That must be Stinky.

I bet he has Cleo."

Clifford and T-Bone

ran back into the woods.

A skunk *did* have Cleo.

But this was no ghost.

This skunk was real—very real.

He left his stinky smell,

then walked away.

T-Bone held his nose
while Clifford set
Cleo free.

"Thanks, guys," Cleo said.

"I'm sorry I played

those tricks on you."

Cleo ran home

and had a bath.

Then she went to

find her friends.